Project Editor Lara Hutcheson
Designers James McKeag, Emma Wicks
Managing Editor Tori Kosara
Managing Art Editor Jo Connor
Production Editor Siu Yin Chan
Senior Production Controller Lloyd Robertson
Publisher Paula Regan
Art Director Charlotte Coulais
Managing Director Mark Searle

DK would like to thank Hank Woon and the rest of the team at The Pokémon Company International.
Thanks also to Kayla Dugger for proofreading and Americanization.

First American Edition, 2025
Published in the United States by DK Publishing,
a division of Penguin Random House LLC
1745 Broadway, 20th Floor, New York, NY 10019

©2025 Pokémon. ©1995–2025 Nintendo / Creatures Inc. / GAME FREAK inc. TM, ®, and character names are trademarks of Nintendo.
25 26 27 28 29 30 10 9 8 7 6 5 4 3 2 1
001–344935–Aug/2025

All rights reserved.
Without limiting the rights under the copyright reserved above, no part of this publication may be reproduced, stored in or introduced into a retrieval system, or transmitted, in any form, or by any means (electronic, mechanical, photocopying, recording, or otherwise), without the prior written permission of the copyright owner.
No part of this publication may be used or reproduced in any manner for the purpose of training artificial intelligence technologies or systems. In accordance with Article 4(3) of the DSM Directive 2019/790, DK expressly reserves this work from the text and data mining exception.

Published in Great Britain by Dorling Kindersley Limited

ISBN 978-0-5939-6589-4

DK books are available at special discounts when purchased in bulk for sales promotions, premiums, fund-raising, or educational use.
For details, contact: DK Publishing Special Markets,
1745 Broadway, 20th Floor, New York, NY 10019
SpecialSales@dk.com

Printed and bound in China

www.dk.com
www.pokemon.com

This book was made with Forest Stewardship Council™ certified paper—one small step in DK's commitment to a sustainable future.
Learn more at www.dk.com/uk/information/sustainability

CONTENTS

SPARKLE AND SHINE
Twinkle time	10
Deck the halls	12
Marvelous music	14

SNUGGLE UP
Festive Fire types	18
Fiery friends	20
Would you rather	22

A FESTIVE FEAST
Tasty treats	26
Find the foods	28
Food fun	30

FUN WITH FRIENDS
Generous gifts	34
Ready to relax	36
Guess the Pokémon	38
The Pokémon are ...	40
Cool companions	42

IT'S SNOW TIME!
Battle buddies	46
Awesome Ice types	48
Fierce and frosty	50

HAPPY HOLIDAYS
Let's dance	54
Playful Pokémon	56
Quaxly's quiz	58
Quiz answers	60

WELCOME

The holidays are finally here, and so are your Pokémon friends from across all the known regions. They are ready to feast, snuggle, have fun—and use their amazing skills to add sparkle to the festive season!

SPARKLE AND SHINE

Many Pokémon can use their awesome skills to spread festive cheer. From displaying pretty lights to singing sweet melodies—their talents will dazzle you!

TWINKLE TIME

These Pokémon add lots of festive sparkle. Ninetales' fur gleams gold, while Glaceon can turn the falling snow into sparkling diamond dust. But for a real light show, gather some Pikachu—it will be electric!

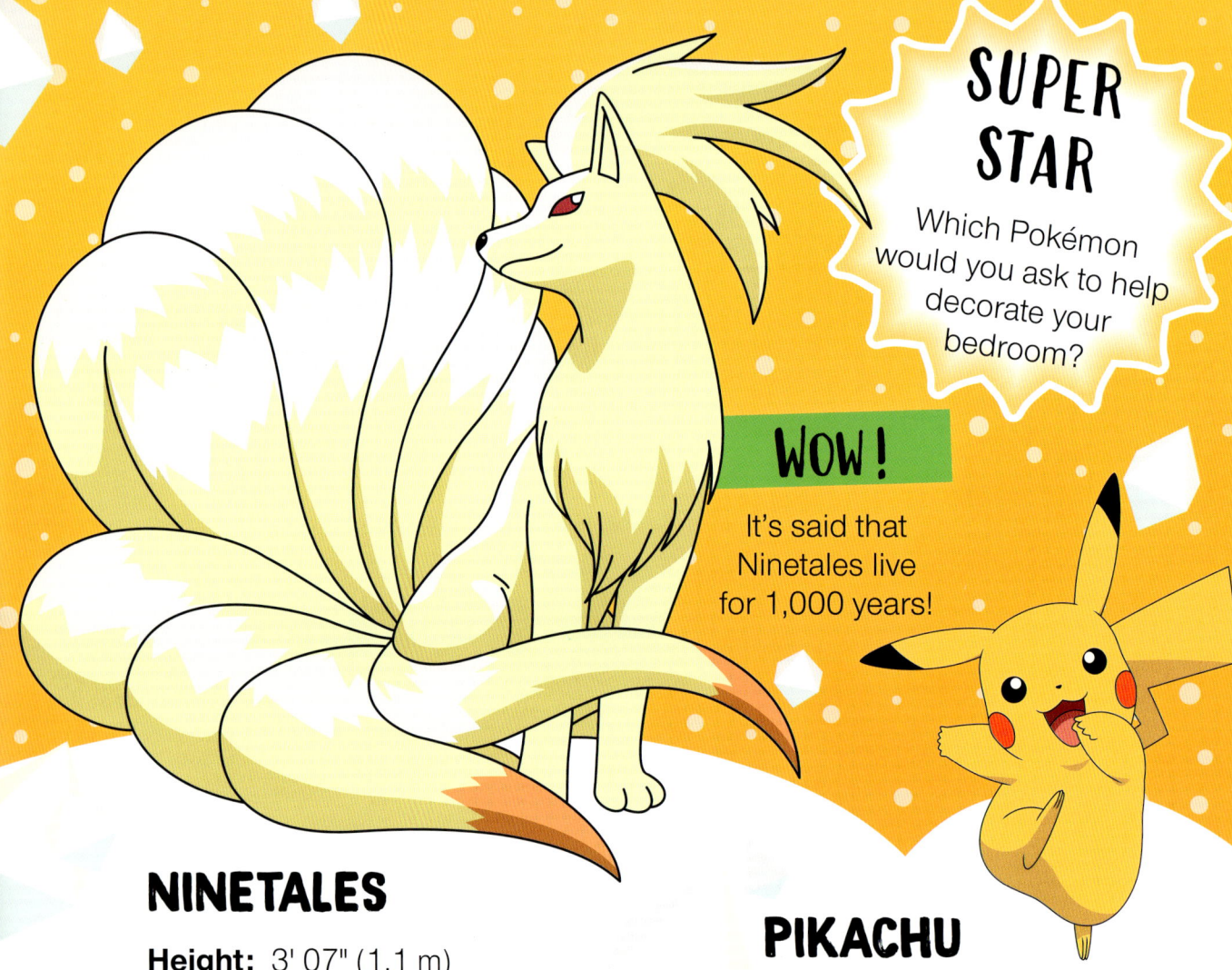

SUPER STAR
Which Pokémon would you ask to help decorate your bedroom?

WOW! It's said that Ninetales live for 1,000 years!

NINETALES
Height: 3' 07" (1.1 m)
Category: Fox
Type: Fire

PIKACHU
Height: 1' 04" (0.4 m)
Category: Mouse
Type: Electric

SO COOL!

Starmie's core can glow in seven colors!

STARMIE

Height: 3' 07" (1.1 m)
Category: Mysterious
Type: Water-Psychic

HO HO HO!

What did Meowth say when the string lights broke?

It's a cat-astrophe!

GLACEON

Height: 2' 07" (0.8 m)
Category: Fresh Snow
Type: Ice

DECK THE HALLS

Mythical Pokémon make everything look special for the holidays. Shaymin spread flowers and Diancie create glimmering diamonds. What decorations would you like? Jirachi will make your wishes come true!

SHAYMIN (LAND FORME)

Height: 1' 04" (0.4 m)
Category: Gratitude
Type: Grass-Flying

WOW!
Shaymin can turn ruined land into a lush field of beautiful flowers!

SUPER STAR
Which mythical Pokémon is your favorite?

DIANCIE

Height: 2' 04" (0.7 m)
Category: Jewel
Type: Rock-Fairy

SO COOL!

Diancie's glimmering body is said to be the lovliest sight in the whole wide world!

HO HO HO!

What did the Pokémon Trainer say when they woke up Jirachi?

"It's a dream come true!"

JIRACHI

Height: 1' (0.3 m)
Category: Wish
Type: Steel-Psychic

MARVELOUS MUSIC

Now it's time for some musical magic. These noisy Pokémon are known for their unique and impressive sounds. Put them all together and you could be on your way to creating a holiday hit!

CHINGLING

Can you hear that ringing sound? It's from the orb in Chingling's mouth as it hops up and down!

Height: 0' 08" (0.2 m)
Category: Bell
Type: Psychic

KRICKETUNE

Kricketune blast the most amazing sound from their bellies. Singing competition anyone?

Height: 3' 03" (1 m)
Category: Cricket
Type: Bug

SUPER STAR

Which Pokémon would you ask to join your band?

MELOETTA
(ARIA FORME)

This **Mythical Pokémon** just loves to sing. Its mighty melodies have the power to make others feel happy or sad.

Height: 2' (0.6 m)
Category: Melody
Type: Normal-Psychic

GROOKEY

Grookey have fun striking with their stick. The more they strike, the more energetic the beat becomes.

Height: 1' (0.3 m)
Category: Chimp
Type: Grass

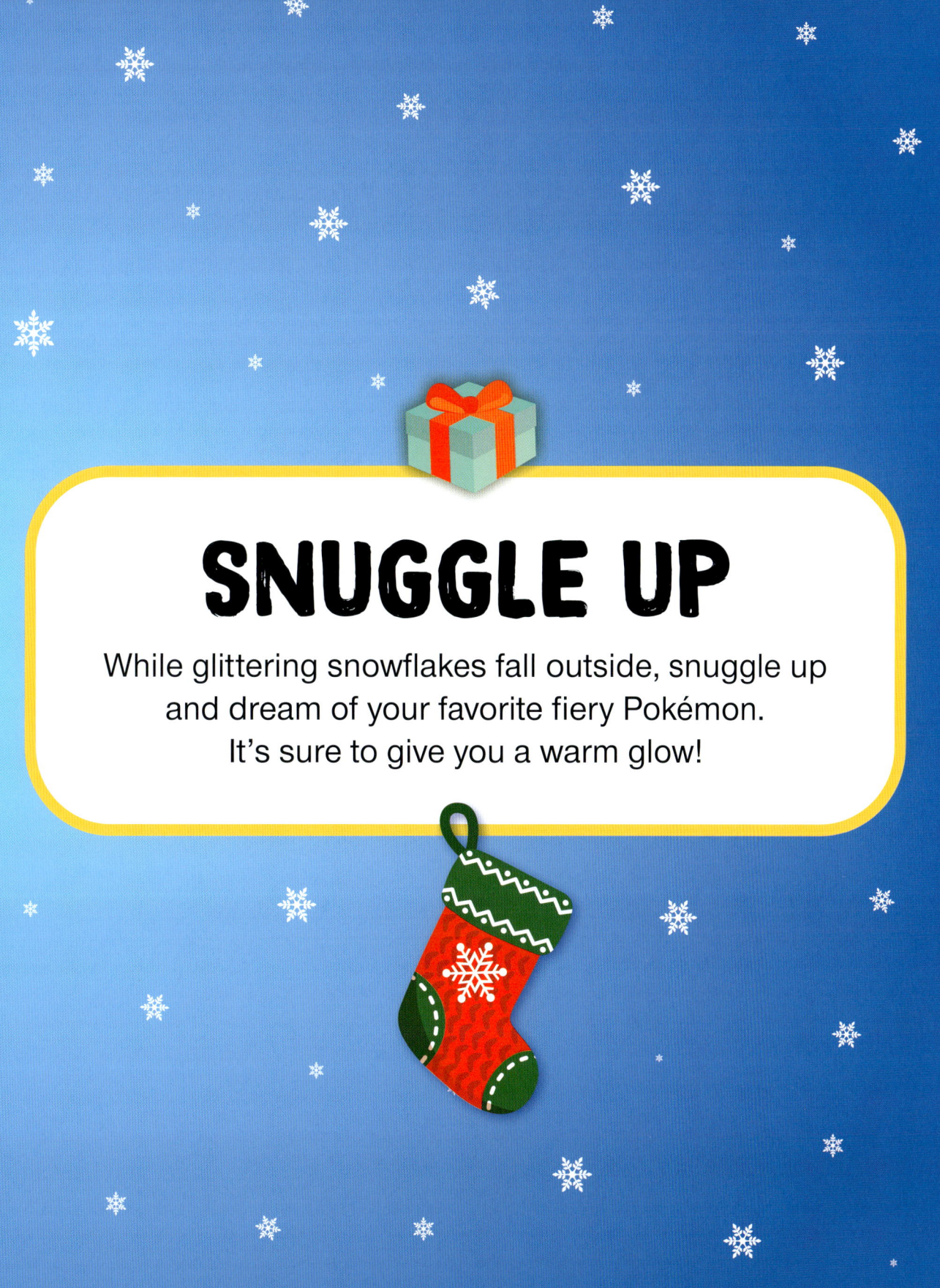

SNUGGLE UP

While glittering snowflakes fall outside, snuggle up and dream of your favorite fiery Pokémon. It's sure to give you a warm glow!

FESTIVE FIRE TYPES

In frosty weather, toasty-warm Fire-type Pokémon are good to have around. Feel the heat from Scorbunny's feet and Fennekin's body, or call on Fuecoco and Cyndaquil to add some sizzle to any celebration!

HO HO HO!

Why is Cyndaquil's cooking inedible?

It's always burnt to a cinder!

CYNDAQUIL

Height: 1' 08" (0.5 m)
Category: Fire Mouse
Type: Fire

WOW!

If Cyndaquil are surprised, flames will shoot from their back. Now that's a shock!

SCORBUNNY

Height: 1' (0.3 m)
Category: Rabbit
Type: Fire

FUECOCO

Height: 1' 04" (0.4 m)
Category: Fire Croc
Type: Fire

FENNEKIN

Height: 1' 04" (0.4 m)
Category: Fox
Type: Fire

SO COOL!

Fennekin get courage from nibbling twigs—so beware a snack attack!

FIERY FRIENDS

Get your Poké Ball at the ready, it's time to catch a fabulous Fire type! These Fire-type Pokémon are perfect for keeping you warm and cozy. Just watch out for any flaming fireballs!

TEPIG

Tepig launch glowing fireballs from their nostrils! If they ever used fire energy to cook you a festive dinner, it would probably be burnt to a crisp.

Height: 1' 08" (0.5 m)
Category: Fire Pig
Type: Fire

TORCHIC

Torchic are never cold, thanks to a sac of burning fire in their belly. If you're feeling the chill, Torchic's toasty hugs will warm you up in no time.

Height: 1' 04" (0.4 m)
Category: Chick
Type: Fire

FLAREON

Fluffy Flareon look cute, but you might not want to get too close. Their body radiates scorching heat and their breath is red-hot fire!

Height: 2' 11" (0.9 m)
Category: Flash Fire
Type: Fire

DARUMAKA

If you have frosty fingers, Darumaka are a good Pokémon to catch. People put Darumaka's hot droppings into their pockets to keep their hands warm!

Height: 2' (0.6 m)
Category: Zen Charm
Type: Fire

HO HO HO!

Why are Darumaka's droppings popular over the holidays?

Because they're the hottest gift around!

WOULD YOU RATHER

To keep the winter chill at bay, let's find a festive game to play. Read the questions, think them through ... which one would you rather do?

WOULD YOU RATHER ...

try snowboarding with Squirtle or sledding with Fennekin?

HO HO HO!

Why did Oshawott cross the road?

To get to Sea Otter side!

WOULD YOU RATHER ...

wrap presents with Pikachu or sing festive songs with Fuecoco?

WOULD YOU RATHER ...

chase snowflakes with Sprigatito or go swimming with Oshawott?

WOULD YOU RATHER ... make an Eevee-shaped cookie or a Snorlax-shaped snow-Pokémon?

WOULD YOU RATHER ... climb up a tree with Treecko or jump over it like Froakie?

WOULD YOU RATHER ... stay up all night with Rowlet or have a little snooze with Smoliv?

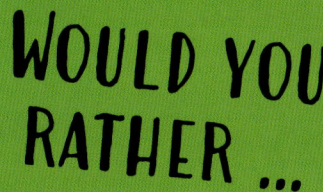

A FESTIVE FEAST

The halls are decked and everything is sparkling. More Pokémon are on the way—they know that a festive feast will make this magical moment complete.

TASTY TREATS

Festive feasts take a lot of time to prepare. Luckily, these food-loving Pokémon can quickly rustle up some tasty treats. Lechonk forages for the finest of foods, while Fidough helps out with the baking!

HO HO HO!

Why do Lechonk like to serve dessert?

Because finding food is a piece of cake!

LECHONK

Height: 1' 08" (0.5 m)
Category: Hog
Type: Normal

SUPER STAR

Which Pokémon would you ask to whip up your festive feast?

WOW!

Delibird never arrive empty-handed. They always carry a sack full of food!

DELIBIRD

Height: 2' 11" (0.9 m)
Category: Delivery
Type: Ice-Flying

SO COOL!

Fidough make bread and cakes rise just by using their breath.

FIDOUGH

Height: 1' (0.3 m)
Category: Puppy
Type: Fairy

FIND THE FOODS

Oh no! In all this merry mayhem, festive foods have scattered all over the place! Can you spot the sweet treats hiding in this picture? Count them up!

FOOD FUN

Are you ready for a merry meal? These Pokémon REALLY love their food! Swirlix want to eat all the sugar, and if there are berries on offer, Skwovet will be happy. As for Yamper and Gulpin—they're not picky!

YAMPER

Height: 1' (0.3 m)
Category: Puppy
Type: Electric

SKWOVET

Height: 1' (0.3 m)
Category: Cheeky
Type: Normal

WOW! Greedy Yamper will only help people in exchange for a tasty treat!

FUN WITH FRIENDS

Nothing spreads cheer more than spending time with friends. Sharing is caring, and many Pokémon have wonderful gifts to offer—from sweet scents to a whole lot of holiday happiness!

GENEROUS GIFTS

It's the season for sharing—and these kind Pokémon are feeling very generous. They can offer you gifts of sweet cream, leaves, berries, and joy! Are they your perfect Pokémon partners?

HO HO HO!

Why do Pansage make such good friends?

They help you leaf all your worries behind!

PANSAGE

These Pokémon love to share! Whether they're giving you the stress-busting leaf from their head or a refreshing berry, Pansage are super kind.

Height: 2' (0.6 m)
Category: Grass Monkey
Type: Grass

SUPER STAR

Which Pokémon would you like as your best friend?

TOGETIC

For an instant dose of holiday cheer, let Togetic shower you with happiness. This floating friend won't let you down!

Height: 2' (0.6 m)
Category: Happiness
Type: Fairy-Flying

ALCREMIE

Make sure to invite Alcremie to your festive feast. These joyful Pokémon decorate desserts with their sweet cream. One taste will make you happy!

Height: 1' (0.3 m)
Category: Cream
Type: Fairy

READY TO RELAX

Pause for a moment to soak up the holiday atmosphere. Let your Pokémon pals help you relax with their sleepy songs, soothing auras, and wonderfully calming scents.

SYLVEON

Height: 3' 04" (1 m)
Category: Intertwining
Type: Fairy

SO COOL!

Sylveon use their flowing, ribbonlike feelers to send out soothing vibes. They can make everyone feel calm.

HO HO HO!

Why wouldn't Jigglypuff make a good music teacher?

Its songs would put the class to sleep!

JIGGLYPUFF

Height: 1' 07" (0.5 m)
Category: Balloon
Type: Normal-Fairy

WOW!

Take a sniff of the garland on Lilligant's head and you'll feel wonderfully relaxed.

LILLIGANT

Height: 3' 07" (1.1 m)
Category: Flowering
Type: Grass

GUESS THE POKÉMON

What's the perfect present for a Pokémon Trainer? A Pokémon! Study the shapes and clues to guess which Pokémon from across the regions have been unwrapped. Turn over for the answers.

A POKÉMON WITH A SHELL FULL OF BERRIES MAKES A GREAT FESTIVE GIFT!

ITS GLOWING RINGS CAN LIGHT UP THE DARKNESS.

THIS POKÉMON'S NAME RHYMES WITH "ANTLER."

QUICK! GUESS WHO'S HERE BEFORE IT EVOLVES INTO A DIFFERENT SPECIES!

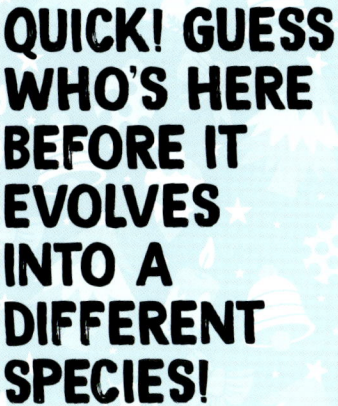

HERE'S A GHOST-TYPE POKÉMON THAT LOOKS LIKE A REAL CU-TEA!

DON'T BE FOOLED— THIS IS NOT A TREE!

KEEP AS COOL AS AN ICE CUBE OVER THE HOLIDAYS WITH THIS PENGUIN POKÉMON.

WOW!

Mimikyu are wrapped in a cloth that looks like Pikachu!

THE POKÉMON ARE ...

The shapes have been uncovered, revealing the Pokémon team inside. Did you guess correctly, or is it a wonderful surprise?

SHUCKLE

Shuckle keeps berries safe in its shell until they turn into a thick juice. Yum!

Height: 2' (0.6 m)
Category: Mold
Type: Bug-Rock

UMBREON

On dark, wintry nights, look out for Umbreon. The moonlight makes its golden rings glow brightly.

Height: 3' 03" (1 m)
Category: Moonlight
Type: Dark

STANTLER

Long ago, Stantler had stronger psychic abilities. It could even evolve under its own power.

Height: 4' 07" (1.4 m)
Category: Big Horn
Type: Normal

EEVEE

Cute and fluffy Eevee can evolve into different species. This skill is useful and often surprising!

Height: 1' (0.3 m)
Category: Evolution
Type: Normal

SINISTEA

A warming cup of tea sounds lovely. But don't drink Sinistea, as it tastes revolting.

Height: 4" (0.1 m)
Category: Black Tea
Type: Ghost

SUDOWOODO

This Rock-type is definitely not a tree. It hates water and runs away from rain!

Height: 3' 11" (1.2 m)
Category: Imitation
Type: Rock

EISCUE

When it's hot outside, groups of Eiscue will hold their heads together to keep cool.

Height: 4' 07" (1.4 m)
Category: Penguin
Type: Ice

HO HO HO!
Why won't Azumarill play hide-and-seek?

They're always spotted!

COOL COMPANIONS

It's great to celebrate friends' talents, so raise a cheer to these rare and powerful **Legendary Pokémon**. They'll make a special day even more dazzling, with awesome skills that are off the charts!

SILVALLY

If you become best friends with Silvally, you might be in for a surprise. This Legendary Pokémon has the power to change its type!

Height: 7' 07" (2.3 m)
Category: Synthetic
Type: Normal

HEATRAN

Have you ever seen Heatran? Well, try looking up! Heatran can use its cross-shaped feet to cleverly crawl along the ceiling!

Height: 5' 07" (1.7 m)
Category: Lava Dome
Type: Fire-Steel

REGIGIGAS

Super-strong, bedecked with gemstones, and able to create Pokémon that look just like it—Regigigas is incredible!

Height: 12' 02" (3.7 m)
Category: Colossal
Type: Normal

RAYQUAZA

This Flying- and Dragon-type is an amazing sight. Rayquaza swirls through the sky, munching on meteorites as it grows even more powerful.

Height: 23' (7 m)
Category: Sky High
Type: Dragon-Flying

IT'S SNOW TIME!

Wrap up warm and dash through the snow with your Pokémon pals. It won't be long before everyone is swept up in flurries of festive joy!

BATTLE BUDDIES

Watch out! These Pokémon friends are ready for a fun snowball fight—and Bulbasaur is taking aim. Thank goodness that the tail flame of a heathly Charmander will burn bright even if it gets a bit wet!

HO HO HO!
Which Pokémon sounds like a sneeze?
Pichu!

BULBASAUR

Height: 2' 04" (0.7 m)
Category: Seed
Type: Grass-Poison

SQUIRTLE

Height: 1' 08" (0.5 m)
Category: Tiny Turtle
Type: Water

SO COOL!

Squirtle's shell is so hard that a snowball would probably bounce right off it!

SUPER STAR

Which Pokémon would you want on your team in a snowball fight?

CHARMANDER

Height: 2' (0.6 m)
Category: Lizard
Type: Fire

47

AWESOME ICE TYPES

Have you ever been so cold that your teeth started chattering? You might not like feeling chilly, but for many Pokémon, being frosty is fabulous! Meet the Ice types who can thrive in cold climates.

SNOM

If Snom see snowflakes, they think it's dinnertime! Snom love to eat snow and can easily munch their way up to the very top of a mountain.

Height: 1' (0.3 m)
Category: Worm
Type: Ice-Bug

ALOLAN VULPIX

Don't offer an Alolan Vulpix your scarf. If this Ice type gets too warm, they might cool down by spraying the air with ice shards.

Height: 2' (0.6 m)
Category: Fox
Type: Ice

HO HO HO!
Why did Cubchoo chase its nose?
Because it was running!

VANILLITE

It's said that this Pokémon was born from an icicle. They spew out freezing air that can make it snow. Watch your step, because you might find one burried in the snow having a little snooze!

Height: 1' 04" (0.4 m)
Category: Fresh Snow
Type: Ice

CUBCHOO

A Cubchoo's dangling snot is a sign of good health, but if they start sneezing, run before you get splattered! Their frosty snot will give you frostbite.

Height: 1' 08" (0.5 m)
Category: Chill
Type: Ice

FIERCE AND FROSTY

Beware these frosty figures and their brrr-illiant moves! Abomasnow whip up sudden blizzards, while Froslass get into the holiday spirit by freezing their foes and hanging them up as decorations. Eek!

GLALIE

Height: 4' 11" (1.5 m)
Category: Face
Type: Ice

WOW!

Glalie freeze their prey with a blast of icy breath. Then they gobble them up!

SUPER STAR

Which Ice-type Pokémon is your favorite?

ABOMASNOW

Height: 7' 03" (2.2 m)
Category: Frost Tree
Type: Grass-Ice

HO HO HO!
What do Ice-type Pokémon love doing most over the holidays?
Chilling with their friends!

FROSLASS

Height: 4' 03" (1.3 m)
Category: Snow Land
Type: Ice-Ghost

REGICE

Height: 5' 11" (21.8 m)
Category: Iceberg
Type: Ice

SO COOL!

Legendary Pokémon
Regice is made of solid ice. It will freeze anything that comes close.

HAPPY HOLIDAYS

Oh what fun it is to party with Pokémon! They can't wait to spread cheer with their dizzying dance moves, cool quiz questions, and surprising talents. Let's get the good times rolling!

LET'S DANCE

If you're heading to the dance floor, then take some tips from these Pokémon. Stomp along to Ludicolo's energetic rhythm, try Mr. Rime's tap dancing, or gracefully move like Masquerain and Primarina.

MR. RIME
Height: 4' 11" (1.5 m)
Category: Comedian
Type: Ice-Psychic

SO COOL!

Fun-loving Ludicolo get their energy from upbeat and cheerful dancing.

LUDICOLO
Height: 4' 11" (1.5 m)
Category: Carefree
Type: Water-Grass

SO COOL!

All eyes are on Masquerain's moves—they can skillfully dip and dive in any direction.

MASQUERAIN
Height: 2' 07" (0.8 m)
Category: Eyeball
Type: Bug-Flying

SUPER STAR
What's your favorite dance move?

PRIMARINA
Height: 5' 11" (1.8 m)
Category: Soloist
Type: Water-Fairy

WOW!

Primarina's dancing and singing is spectacular—and powerful. It can be used to defeat enemies in battle!

HO HO HO!
Why is tap dancing dangerous?
You might fall into the sink!

55

PLAYFUL POKÉMON

What's better than spending the festive season with your friends? Spending it with your Pokémon pals, too! These entertaining, playful Pokémon are ready to delight. They're sure to add fun to any party.

SKITTY

Adorable Skitty chase their tails around and around until they get dizzy. This silly sight will have you smiling all day.

Height: 2' (0.6 m)
Category: Kitten
Type: Normal

RIBOMBEE

Little Ribombee can sense if you're feeling sad. They'll flutter over with a handmade pollen puff to cheer you up.

Height: 0' 08" (0.2 m)
Category: Bee Fly
Type: Bug-Fairy

SUPER STAR

Which Pokémon makes you laugh the most?

POPPLIO

How's this for an impressive party trick—Popplio can blow cool water bubbles out of their noses. Watch as they get bigger ... and bigger!

Height: 1' 04" (0.4 m)
Category: Sea Lion
Type: Water

MR. MIME

These pantomime experts are very entertaining. Mr. Mime are able to create walls that are real but also invisible!

Height: 4' 03" (1.3 m)
Category: Barrier
Type: Psychic-Fairy

HO HO HO!

Why didn't Mr. Mime help out with the festive feast? It was just miming its own business!

QUAXLY'S QUIZ

Quiz the season to be jolly! You have sparkled, snuggled, and partied with Pokémon. Now it's time to take Quaxly's quiz to discover how much you've merrily learned along the way.

1 WHICH ICE-TYPE POKÉMON CAN TURN FALLING SNOW INTO DIAMOND DUST?

2 DO SYLVEON SEND SOOTHING VIBES THROUGH THEIR NOSES?

3 WHAT IS THE NAME OF THIS POKÉMON?

4 WHAT DOES A DELIBIRD ALWAYS CARRY?

5 WILL THE FLAME ON A HEALTHY CHARMANDER'S TAIL GO OUT IF IT GETS WET?

6 DOES FUECOCO'S HEAD RELEASE FIRE ENERGY OR AN ICE JET?

7 MIMIKYU HIDE UNDER A CLOTH THAT RESEMBLES WHICH ELECTRIC-TYPE POKÉMON?

8 WHAT HAPPENS IF CYNDAQUIL ARE SURPRISED?

HO HO HO!
How did Quaxly avoid being hit by a snowball?
It ducked!

9 WHICH BIG HORN POKÉMON CAN EVOLVE UNDER ITS OWN POWER?

10 CAN CUBCHOO'S SNOT GIVE YOU FROSTBITE?

QUIZ ANSWERS

Did you spot all the sweet treats and remember the Pokémon facts? It's time to find out!

PAGES 28-29 FIND THE FOODS

 9 Lollipops
 4 Rawst Berries
 3 Leppa Berries
 3 Magost Berries
 2 Pikachu cookies
 2 Eevee cookies
 4 Candy canes
 4 Candies

PAGES 58–59 QUAXLY'S QUIZ

1. Glaceon.
2. No. They use their feelers.
3. Fidough.
4. A sack full of food.
5. No. It will burn brightly even if it gets wet.
6. Fire energy.
7. Pikachu.
8. Flames shoot from their back.
9. Stantler.
10. Yes.

Your score

Give yourself one point for every question you answered correctly. What is you score?

0—3 points

Good effort. Give it another try and you'll be a pro in no time!

4—7 points

Sparkling skills! Your Pokémon knowledge is very impressive.

8—10 points

Sleigh to go! Congratulations, you are a true Pokémon expert!